頑皮一族

Lucy Kincaid 著

Gill Guile 繪

曾蕙蘭 譯

三民書局

Read by Myself   ISBN 1 85854 514 5

Written by Lucy Kincaid and illustrated by Gill Guile

First published in 1996

Under the title Read by Myself

by Brimax Books Limited

4/5 Studlands Park Ind. Estate,

Newmarket, Suffolk, CB8 7AU

牧羊犬山姆
Sam the Sheep-dog

Sam the sheep-dog is trying to **herd** the sheep into their pen. But they will not go in! Five sheep are in the **wheelbarrow**. Three sheep are asleep in the hay. All the others are playing games in the **field**.

There are no sheep in the pen. "I am not a very good sheep-dog," says Sam.

herd [hɝd]
動 聚集

wheelbarrow [ˋhwil͵bæro]
名 手推車

field [fild]
名 田野

牧ㄇㄨˋ羊ㄧㄤˊ犬ㄑㄩㄢˇ山ㄕㄢ姆ㄇㄨˇ想ㄒㄧㄤˇ要ㄧㄠˋ把ㄅㄚˇ羊ㄧㄤˊ群ㄑㄩㄣˊ趕ㄍㄢˇ到ㄉㄠˋ圍ㄨㄟˊ欄ㄌㄢˊ裡ㄌㄧˇ，可ㄎㄜˇ是ㄕˋ他ㄊㄚ們ㄇㄣ不ㄅㄨˋ想ㄒㄧㄤˇ進ㄐㄧㄣˋ去ㄑㄩˋ。有ㄧㄡˇ五ㄨˇ隻ㄓ羊ㄧㄤˊ在ㄗㄞˋ手ㄕㄡˇ推ㄊㄨㄟ車ㄔㄜ裡ㄌㄧˇ；有ㄧㄡˇ三ㄙㄢ隻ㄓ羊ㄧㄤˊ在ㄗㄞˋ乾ㄍㄢ草ㄘㄠˇ堆ㄉㄨㄟ上ㄕㄤˋ睡ㄕㄨㄟˋ覺ㄐㄧㄠˋ；其ㄑㄧˊ他ㄊㄚ的ㄉㄜ羊ㄧㄤˊ則ㄗㄜˊ在ㄗㄞˋ田ㄊㄧㄢˊ野ㄧㄝˇ上ㄕㄤˋ玩ㄨㄢˊ遊ㄧㄡˊ戲ㄒㄧˋ。

圍ㄨㄟˊ欄ㄌㄢˊ裡ㄌㄧˇ沒ㄇㄟˊ有ㄧㄡˇ半ㄅㄢˋ隻ㄓ羊ㄧㄤˊ。「我ㄨㄛˇ不ㄅㄨˋ是ㄕˋ一ㄧ隻ㄓ優ㄧㄡ秀ㄒㄧㄡˋ的ㄉㄜ牧ㄇㄨˋ羊ㄧㄤˊ犬ㄑㄩㄢˇ。」山ㄕㄢ姆ㄇㄨˇ說ㄕㄨㄛ。

The next day, Sam wakes early. "It is the Sheep **Show** today," he says to Dolly Donkey. "All the sheep must have a **bath**. They might **win** a **prize**." The big **bathtub** is filled with soapy water. Sam goes to **fetch** the sheep from the field.

"I will help," says Dolly.

第二天，山姆早早就醒來了。「今天是綿羊大展的日子。」他對驢子桃莉說。「全部的綿羊都得洗個澡。他們也許會得獎呢！」

大澡盆裡滿滿的肥皂水。山姆到田野上要把綿羊趕過來。

「我來幫忙。」桃莉說。

5

But the sheep will not go near the bathtub.

"Please go in the water," says Sam. But the sheep go in the pig-pen **instead**. They **roll** in the mud with the pigs and soon their white coats are very dirty.

"Oh dear," says Sam. "I am not a very good sheep-dog."

"I will also help to herd the sheep," says Curly Piglet.

instead [ɪn`stɛd]
副 反而

roll [rol]
動 滾來滾去

可是綿羊們不肯靠近澡盆一步。
「洗個澡好嗎？」山姆說。可是綿羊們反而進到豬圈裡去了。他們和豬隻在泥巴裡翻滾，一會兒就把身上弄得髒兮兮的。
「喔！天啊！」山姆說。「我不是一隻優秀的牧羊犬。」
「我也來幫你趕羊。」小豬捲毛說。

The sheep run away! They do not go near the big bathtub. They go inside the **henhouse** and sit in the **straw** with the hens.

"Oh dear," says Sam. "Now they have straw and mud on them. They will never be **clean** for the Sheep Show."

"I will help you to herd the sheep," says Cassie Calf.

henhouse [ˋhɛn͵haʊs]
名 雞舍

straw [strɔ]
名 稻草

clean [klin]
形 清潔的

綿羊們跑掉了！他們就是不肯靠近那個大澡盆。他們跑進了雞舍，跟著母雞坐在草堆裡。

「喔！天啊！」山姆說。「他們身上全是稻草和泥巴，到綿羊大展時，是絕不會變乾淨的。」

「我來幫你趕羊。」小牛凱西說。

But the sheep still will not go into the bathtub. They go out of the henhouse and past the pig-pen. They go across to the **duck pond** and **splash** in the **muddy** water. Now they are even dirtier!

duck [dʌk]
名 鴨子

pond [pɑnd]
名 池塘

splash [splæʃ]
動 潑濺

muddy [ˋmʌdɪ]
形 泥濘的

可是綿羊們還是不想進到澡盆裡。他們跑出了雞舍，經過豬圈。他們穿過鴨塘，還在泥水裡潑水玩耍。現在的他們更髒了！

"Please **climb** into the bathtub," says Cassie Calf. But the sheep go out of the farmyard and across the fields. They **wave** to the **scarecrow** and go through the **gate**. They go down the **lane** and soon come to the park.

climb [klaɪm]
動 爬

wave [wev]
動 揮手

scarecrow [`skɛr,kro]
名 稻草人

gate [get]
名 大門

lane [len]
名 小路

「拜託進澡盆吧！」小牛凱西說。可是綿羊們卻跑出農院，穿過了田野。他們向稻草人招了招手，出了柵門。他們走下小路，不久就來到了公園。

"This looks fun," say the sheep. They climb to the **top** of the slide and **slide** all the way down. Then they play on the **swings**.

"We must go home now," says Sam. "It is nearly time for the Sheep Show." But the sheep are having too much fun.

top [tɑp]
名 頂端

slide [slaɪd]
名 滑梯 動 滑

swing [swɪŋ]
名 鞦韆

「這看起來好好玩喲！」綿羊們說。他們爬到溜滑梯頂端，玩起了溜滑梯。他們還玩了盪鞦韆。

「我們現在必須回家了，」山姆說。「綿羊大展的時間快到了。」可是綿羊們正玩得起勁呢！

They play **tennis** and have a **ride** on a little train. They have an ice-cream, but it **melts** and **sticks** to them. They play in the **sandbox** and the sand sticks to them as well.

"Oh dear," says Sam. "They have mud, straw, ice-cream and sand stuck to them!"

tennis [ˋtɛnɪs]
名 網球

ride [raɪd]
名 乘坐

melt [mɛlt]
動 融化

stick [stɪk]
動 黏

sandbox [ˋsænd͵bɑks]
名 沙坑

他們打網球，還坐在一列小火車上兜風。他們吃著冰淇淋，可是冰融化了，黏在他們身上。他們在沙坑裡玩耍，而沙子也沾滿他們全身。

「喔！天啊！」山姆說。「泥巴、稻草、冰淇淋，還有沙子，全都黏到他們身上了！」

"We must go home," says Sam. The sheep run past the slide and the swings. They wave to the little train and **trot** through the sandbox. They run across the **grass** and into a **fountain**!

"Oh dear," says Sam. "I am not a very good sheep-dog."

trot [trɑt]
勔 快跑

grass [græs]
名 草地

fountain [ˈfaʊntn̩]
名 噴水池

「我們得回家了。」山姆說。
綿羊們跑過溜滑梯和鞦韆。他們向小火車招了招手，然後跑過沙坑。他們越過草地，跑進了一座噴水池中！
「喔！天啊！」山姆說。「我不是一隻優秀的牧羊犬。」

The sheep stand under the **cool** water.

"They are having a **shower**," says Cassie Calf. The mud, straw, ice-cream and sand is soon washed away. The sheep are clean and white once more.

"Now we do not need a bath," they say. They walk home to the farm. On the way they see the Sheep Show, they go inside.

綿羊們站在清涼的池水下。

「他們正在洗澡呢！」小牛凱西說。泥巴、稻草、冰淇淋和沙子很快就被洗掉了。綿羊們又變得乾淨潔白了呢！

「現在我們不需要洗澡了。」他們說。他們走向農場要回家。半路上，他們看到綿羊大展就進去了。

There are black sheep with big horns, white sheep with black faces, big sheep and little sheep. There are happy sheep, **sad** sheep, fat sheep and thin sheep. But the **judge** gives first prize to Sam's sheep for being the cleanest. They are all given red **ribbons** and Sam is given a big **silver** cup.

sad [sæd]
形 悲傷的

judge [dʒʌdʒ]
名 評審

ribbon [ˋrɪbən]
名 緞帶

silver [ˋsɪlvɚ]
形 銀的

那裡有大角黑綿羊、黑面白綿羊、大綿羊和小綿羊。有快樂的綿羊、悲傷的綿羊、胖綿羊和瘦綿羊。可是評審把首獎頒給了山姆的綿羊，因為他們是最乾淨的綿羊。評審頒給他們紅色的緞帶，頒給山姆一座大銀杯。

They walk home feeling very happy.
"Where have you been?" asks Tommy
the Cat. "The bath water is cold and
you have **missed** the Sheep Show."
"No we have not," says Sam. "The
sheep won first prize!"
The clean, white, **fluffy** sheep smile.
"We had a lovely day out as well,"
they say.

miss [mɪs]
動 錯過

fluffy [ˈflʌfɪ]
形 毛茸茸的

他們非常快樂地走回家。
「你們去哪兒了？」貓咪湯米問。
「洗澡水都冷了，你們也錯過了綿羊大展！」
「我們可沒錯過喲！」山姆說。「這群綿羊還贏得了首獎呢！」
這些乾淨、潔白、毛茸茸的綿羊笑咪咪地說：「我們一起在外頭享受了愉快的一天呢！」

Everyone is happy. Sam is given a big, **juicy bone** for dinner. The sheep **wear** their ribbons all the time and Sam keeps the big silver cup by his bed.

"We think you are a very good sheep-dog, **after all**," says Cassie Calf.

"So do I," says Sam, **licking** his bone. "So do I!"

juicy [ˈdʒusɪ]
形 多汁的

bone [bon]
名 骨頭

wear [wɛr]
動 戴著

after all
終究，畢竟

lick [lɪk]
動 舔

大夥兒都很高興。山姆得到一支大又多汁的骨頭當晚餐。綿羊們一直戴著他們的緞帶，山姆則把這座大銀杯擺在他的床邊。

「你終究是一隻優秀的牧羊犬！」小牛凱西說。

「我也是這樣想的。」山姆邊說，邊舔著他的骨頭。「我也是這樣想的啊！」

Say these words again.

herd	asleep
wakes	soapy
roll	dirty
clean	climb
slide	having
melts	play
sticks	stand

What can you see?

wheelbarrow

scarecrow

slide

fountain

silver cup

中英對照，既可學英語又可了解偉人小故事哦！

超級科學家系列
SUPER SCIENTISTS

當彗星掠過哈雷眼前，
當蘋果落在牛頓頭頂，
當電燈泡在愛迪生手中亮起……
一個個求知的心靈與真理所碰撞出的火花，
就是《超級科學家系列》！

光的顏色
牛頓的故事

爆炸性的發現
諾貝爾的故事

命運的彗星
哈雷的故事

電燈的發明
愛迪生的故事

望遠天際
伽利略的故事

蠶寶寶的祕密
巴斯德的故事

宇宙教授
愛因斯坦的故事

神祕元素
居禮夫人的故事

神祕元素：居禮夫人的故事
電燈的發明：愛迪生的故事
望遠天際：伽利略的故事
光的顏色：牛頓的故事
爆炸性的發現：諾貝爾的故事
蠶寶寶的祕密：巴斯德的故事
宇宙教授：愛因斯坦的故事
命運的彗星：哈雷的故事

網際網路位址　http : // www. sanmin. com. tw

ⓒ 牧羊犬山姆

著作人　Lucy Kincaid
繪圖者　Gill Guile
譯　者　曾蕙蘭
發行人　劉振強
著作財
產權人　三民書局股份有限公司
　　　　臺北市復興北路三八六號
發行所　三民書局股份有限公司
　　　　地址／臺北市復興北路三八六號
　　　　電話／二五〇〇六六〇〇
　　　　郵撥／〇〇〇九九九八——五號
印刷所　三民書局股份有限公司
門市部　復北店／臺北市復興北路三八六號
　　　　重南店／臺北市重慶南路一段六十一號
初　版　中華民國八十八年十一月
編　號　S85537
定　價　新臺幣壹佰陸拾元整
行政院新聞局登記證局版臺業字第〇二〇〇號

有著作權　不准侵害

ISBN　957-14-3088-9（精裝）

牧羊犬山姆